Buttered up

I have been living with the brunette goddess Victoria for about three years now. The entire time that we have been living together. She has had a boyfriend. So, I have pretty much left her sexy ass alone.

So, this Saturday morning when she brought me breakfast in bed consisting of Tea, whole wheat toast, scrambled eggs and bacon. I was very surprised that she was wearing a completely translucent night gown.

I said good morning, Victoria, this is a surprise. She said what a roommate can't bring her favorite guy breakfast in bed. I said but you have never done it before, and we have been living together for three years. Victoria said there is a first time for everything.

Good thing I was under the covers because Victoria was killing it in that sexy night gown. I could see her perfect C size breast and well-groomed black bush. My flag stick was at full attention and saluting Miss Victoria as she produced her million-dollar smile bringing me breakfast in bed.

I said thank you Victoria for the wonderful gesture. I do appreciate it a lot and she said you're welcome. I said I'm hungry, I dug into the breakfast, and it was very good. Victoria is a wonderful cook when she wants to be and I'm happy for it being so.

I scarfed that breakfast down like a hungry man getting his last meal before his execution. When I was done, Victoria said that she has this Christmas party at a night club coming up and she didn't want to go alone.

I said what about your boyfriend Victor. Victoria said I asked him to go with me, but he declined says he doesn't like public dancing or public displays of affection. I said that bastard, Victoria said I know right. Anyways would you come to my company Christmas party and pretend to be my boyfriend.

I said wow Victoria that is a big ask. She said I know I would really appreciate it and as an incentive. I can wear sexier clothes around the apartment for your viewing pleasure. I said in that case, I would be happy to be your fake boyfriend at your company's Christmas party.

She said oh my god you will do it, I said yes. I can't very well say no after such an exquisite breakfast. I look forward to being your fake boyfriend. I said when is the party? She said tonight.

I said well then, we both went through my walk-in closet to find something suitable to wear for the occasion. Victoria was happy to pick out my clothes for tonight's party. I was very happy to let her pick them out for me.

Victoria was all smiles, all day then it was time to get ready for the party. I shaved, showered and got ready. I was waiting for Victoria to make her grand entrance and wow she did not disappoint. I've never seen her look as lovely as she does tonight in a sexy little black dress.

I said my dear Victoria, you are a breathtaking brunette goddess and I'm delighted to be your boyfriend for the evening. Victoria took my hand

and said thank you for the kind words boyfriend. I said shall we go now, and she said we shall indeed.

I said I'll drive since you are wearing those sexy high heels tonight. Victoria said I think that would be best if you drove. We climbed into my Audi E-Tron GT and took off to the rented-out night club.

Victoria showed our tickets and we entered. It was packed, I said wow didn't know her tech company had these many people on its payroll. We mingled with a lot of Victoria's friends. I was happy that she introduced me as her boyfriend even if it was a lie.

We sat down to eat and drink some fine ass food, I thought this was a very well catered event and first-class treatment. After we ate, Victoria said come on boyfriend let's dance and show them how it's done. I was all too happy to dance with Victoria and her tight sexy body.

When we got to the dance floor, Victoria held me tight, and we danced smiling at each other the whole time. She said thanks for doing this for me, I really appreciate this more than you know. I said my pleasure, Victoria.

Victoria's favorite Britney Spears song came on and she started grinding her pussy on my cock. I was very happy to grind back on her. When I became hard as a rock, I was happy to let her feel my bone. Victoria held me even tighter when I got hard, and I fucking loved it. I held her hips firmer and really gave it to her good.

After a few songs, Victoria turned around so I can grind my hard cock on her sexy bubble butt. My hard cock was between her cheeks, and we were both happy as a clam with a pearl. Victoria and I were in our own little world grinding on each other all night.

When it was over, we were both tired and horny to the max. We said warm goodbyes to her friends at work, one by one then left to head back to our apartment. When we got home, Victoria hugged me tight and said thank you so much for doing this for me. I owe you big time for this one.

I said you're welcome that is when she gave me a quick but stimulating kiss on the lips. We both smiled and said good night, see you in the morning. I went to bed for the first time totally in love with my roommate Victoria.

I woke up early Sunday and made us both coffees. Victoria came in and said that smells so good. I made her favorite coffee that is really expensive. She hugged me tight and gave me a kiss on the lips. We held each other and drank our coffee looking out the window unto Silicon Valley where we work.

Both of us are software engineers from Cal Tech. Victoria and I both graduated with a significant amount of student loan debt. After coffee, I checked my work email and answered a few whiles Victoria did the same. Later, I sat on the couch watching television.

Victoria came to hang out with me closer than normal. She took my arm and put it around her neck, so I held her close as we watched television. After the Christmas party, Victoria is definitely more affectionate with me and I fucking love it even if she has a boyfriend.

Monday we both went to work at different tech companies as competitors. After work, I was on the couch watching television when Victoria in a big t-shirt exposing her sweet white thighs to my watchful eyes. She snuggled up to me rubbing my chest and arms of which I did not mind.

Victoria said my girlfriends at work asked about you today. I said really why would they ask about me. She said they are captivated by your muscles, and she ran her hands all over my chest, arms and six pack in the most sensual of manner.

We continued watching television when Victoria asked if I would give her a back massage. I said sure that is when she took off her t-shirt revealing her perfect breasts to me and red thong. She laid on the couch and I was very happy to massage her back for her. I enjoyed the erotic view of her sexy ass in a thong massaging every inch of her tense back getting all of the knots out.

After I finished massaging her, she hugged me tight bare tits on chest for a long time then she went to her room. I was hooked on sweet miss Victoria. Tuesday morning, Victoria came to the kitchen in a tank top that barely covered her perky wonderful tits, I saw under boob, sweet white thighs and her sexy ass in a blue thong.

I gave her coffee and we sat facing each other. When Victoria raised her cup to take her first sip of coffee, her tank top rode up and revealed her nipples and more of her breast to my watchful eyes. It went back down to cover her tits when she put the cup down on the table. It was a peek a boo heaven the entire time she sipped her coffee. I never enjoyed watching someone drink coffee this much in my life.

When we were finished Victoria hugged me and gave me a peck on the lips saying time to go to work. I said oh yeah, see you later girlfriend as she jiggled her sexy ass away. I went to work horny as hell and came home horny. I went to bed early that night but couldn't sleep.

I heard a knock on the door. I opened my bedroom door with the remote from my nightstand. I said come in and it was Victoria totally naked for the first time. I could see her sweet black bush, perky tits and sweet white thighs. She had a smile on her pretty face then she said in a sexy voice, can you give me another massage.

I said sure Victoria, but I must warn you, I'm naked under the covers. She said its ok, I don't mind you massaging me naked. I said ok then lay down and I'll massage your back for you. She laid down and I started massaging her back admiring her sweet ass and white pussy.

I was massaging her, but my cock was massaging her too. I massaged her for a while and when I was done, Victoria turned over and said since I made you hard can I give you a hand job as a thank you for massaging me.

I said sure Victoria. I was perpendicular to her with my hard-black cock hovering over her bush when she started stroking my black pole. Victoria said you have a really nice big black cock. I moaned thank you Victoria as she stroked my bone really good.

Victoria was all smiles as she stroked the hell out of my hard cock. Ten minutes in and I said oh god here it comes. Victoria aimed my cock at her bush, and I ejaculated all over her bush. I said oh wow all my sperm is in your bush. She said so warm and feels so good in my bush. I said my pleasure thank you so much for the hand job.

Victoria said happy to make you cum and thanks for creaming my bush I really like that a lot. I said you're welcome and she giggled. Victoria said can I stay here tonight. I said sure baby no problem. Facing each other we smiled and went to sleep. We woke up early, I went to the bathroom naked to brush my teeth.

Victoria came into the bathroom and said can I use your shower. I need to wash your sperm out of my bush just in case I see my boyfriend. He might wonder what that is in my bush. I said sure wash your bush in my shower. I watched Victoria in the mirror as she showered soaping up her bush and the rest of her hot body.

I turned around to watch her shower and she said oh no your big cock is hard again; do you want another hand job. I said sure baby, Victoria said come in the shower with me and I'll stroke your nice big dick. I went into the shower for my hand job. Victoria started stroking and I said can I play with your tits. She said go for it, baby. I massaged her tits, as we both moaned with pleasure. I said you have the most perfect tits ever and she smiled at me.

I told her oh god I'm going to come. She aimed it at her bush again, so I shot her in the bush again but this time she rubbed my cock head stroking it in her bush. Damn it was beyond erotic. We finished up our shower and went to work because we were both running later due to erotic shower shenanigans.

Later that night, I waited in bed with my door open this time. Victoria knocked on the door and I said come in. She came in totally naked again and I was happy. Victoria said can I get another massage. I said sure baby and I uncovered my naked body for her viewing pleasure. She had the biggest smile on her pretty face as she laid face down.

I started massaging her back, the upper back first near the shoulder blade then the lower back to admire her sexy ass and pussy which looked wet. My cock pulsed as it rubbed on her sweet ass. Ten minutes later when I finish massaging her back. Victoria turned over and said oh no I made you hard again. I said its ok you always make me hard. Victoria said that's music to my ears then she said do you want to penetrate my bush with your big black dick and make us both feel good.

I said I thought you'd never ask, and Victoria giggled loudly. I rubbed my cock head up and down her slit and all over her sexy black bush. It was very stimulating, and I could feel Victoria's wetness. I tried to push my whole cock into Victoria, and it wouldn't go into her pussy. She said wow your dick is so big it's not going into my tight pussy. I said I have lube. I grabbed the bottle and coated my cock with it then I rubbed it on Victoria's pussy.

I forced my black cock into Victoria's tight white pussy. She said wow I feel totally full like never before and I started massaging her pussy with my cock. We both moaned with pleasure. I fucked her harder and Victoria said oh yeah black man, fuck that white pussy. I said oh yeah white girl, take this black dick. I fucked her harder and she said oh god I'm cumming on your big dick. She coated my whole cock with her warm pussy cream. I said oh yeah, I'm glad I made you cum. She said your turn then bent over. I enter her again holding her sexy wide hips. I pounded her pussy with no mercy until I felt the tingle in my balls then release the kraken.

I ejaculated all of my warm sperm into Victoria. I smacked her sexy ass and said damn that felt good as shit. Victoria said oh wow I finally gave it up to a black stud. I said oh yeah. Victoria turned around and French kissed me really good. So good we both fell over to the bed.

Victoria said by the way I'm never giving you up so don't even think of getting a girlfriend, I'll run her off just so you know. I said yes boss and she laughed out loud. The next morning, I woke up to Victoria's warm pussy on my cock riding me. I woke up and grabbed her tits immediately as she fucked me for breakfast. I said good morning my white lover and she said good morning my black lover. I had to get your black pole in my pink hole before work. I said I love morning pussy and she came all over my cock and a few seconds later. I filled her with my warm cream. We kissed and took a sexy shower together soaping each other up. We got ready, hugged and kissed each other goodbye then went to work.

Months into my sexual relationship with the lovely Victoria. I was in my office working when I got a call on my land line that someone was here to see me. I said who is it and the front desk said she says her name is Victoria. I said send her up immediately please.

I waited until there was a knock on the door, and I opened it, dragged her pretty ass into my office and closed the door immediately locking it. Victoria kissed me and said I just had to see you baby. I said it's great to see you too as I admired her in a sexy zip up dress. I said wow you look amazing baby. She said just bought this I know how you like these kinds of dresses.

I said I love when you dress sexy it turns me on. Victoria unzipped her dress and there was nothing under it. She unzipped my pants and took my hard-black cock out then she dragged me to the couch in my office. Victoria laid down on the couch and said fucked my white pussy with your black cock. I jumped on her sexy ass and rammed my cock all the way up her horny wet cunt. I started pumping and she held me tight. I fucked the shit out of Victoria. She screamed in my mouth when she came then I screamed in her mouth when I flooded her white pussy with my sperm. I said oh wow that was intense baby. I was still in Victoria when there was a knock on the door. I said who is it, and she said its Sarah.

I said oh shit it's my boss. I put my dick away and Victoria put her dress back on quickly. I ran to the door to open it and I said hi, boss, sorry about that my girlfriend was visiting and I locked the door. Sarah walked in and I closed the door. Victoria put her hand out and said it's nice to meet my boyfriend's boss.

Sarah looked my girlfriend up and down then said I think your boyfriend's sperm escaped your pussy and is running down your thighs. I was mortified then Sarah said were you two fucking on the company's time. I said yeah sorry boss, I can't seem to say no to white pussy.

Then Sarah shocked the hell out of both of us when she said I believe the proper place for a black man's cock is in a white woman's tight pussy. Victoria laughed out loud and so did I. I was not expecting that, Sarah giggled and said its ok just be careful fucking on the company's dime. Everyone is not as naughty as I am.

Victoria said I like your boss and hugged her. Two hot white bitches hugging so hot. Victoria said I've caused enough trouble for one day. She hugged me and kissed me as I felt up her ass with the boss watching. Victoria left and it was just Sarah and I in my office.

Sarah said now where is my monthly report. I picked up the monthly report off my desk and gave it to my boss Sarah. She said now that your girlfriend is gone, give your boss a proper greeting. I hugged her tight, French kissed her good and felt up her big juicy ass. Sarah said now that's more like it, does your girlfriend know that you pounded my white pussy with your big black cock.

I said oh god no that is our dirty little secret. Sarah held my face and said good boy, we can't have that getting out because my husband would divorce me, and the company would fire me for not disclosing our sexual affair.

I said yes boss, I know, and I said I'll protect you. Sarah said that's good, I'm happy that you've found a girlfriend who loves cock as much as I do. I said thanks smiling at her and I said you're wet and horny aren't you, Sarah. She said yeah then she reached out and grabbed my hard cock.

Sarah said do you want to fuck me with your dirty cock that you just took out of your girlfriend's wet pussy. I said hell yeah. Sarah jumped on the couch, hiked up her skirt and pulled her panties to the side. I forced my black dick into her horny white pussy. I started hammering her pussy like an animal.

Sarah whispered oh my god I missed you stud as she creamed my black cock. I said wow you came already. I gave it to her harder and I kissed her as I exploded into her married pussy. Sarah said thanks baby I really needed that today. We kissed and held each other. Sarah fixed her panties saying that will keep your sperm in my wet pussy instead of coming out like your girlfriend. I said very true. I pulled down her skirt and put away my cock.

We hugged and kissed then went back to work. I had to take a shower at work before I went home to Victoria. She had some news when I got home. She said my mother is coming to visit and I told her that I broke up with my other boyfriend.

I said so she knows you have a new black boyfriend now. Victoria said she does, and I sent her pictures of us together. She thinks you're hot, I smiled and said when is she coming to visit us. Victoria said my mom is coming next week.

I said wow that's going to come up on us fast. Victoria said my mom is very touchy feely, she will probably hug and kiss you a lot while she is here. I said ok, you mean on the cheeks, Victoria said ah no on the lips, she kisses me on the lips. I said ok that's fine.

A week later we went to the San Jose Airport to pick up her mom. When Victoria saw her mom, they hugged and kissed each other lovingly. Victoria said this is my mom Veronica meet my boyfriend. Veronica said he is so handsome and muscular then she hugged me and kissed me on the lips.

It is amazing how much Veronica and Victoria look alike they could be sisters, wow. We took her luggage to the car. We climbed in the car and went to our apartment. I took all of Veronica's stuff to Victoria's room.

We settled in and Veronica made us all dinner. It was very nice of her to do. We sat and ate dinner together. I listened as Veronica and Victoria caught up on things. Her mom asked how come you broke up with your previous boyfriend.

Victoria said he bailed on my company's Christmas party. My new boyfriend stepped in for him and I knew I had to let my old boyfriend go. Victoria said as soon as I felt my black boyfriend's big cock at my company's Christmas party, I couldn't go back to a smaller cock and someone who won't go out in public with me.

Veronica said I'm happy that you have a guy who pleases you. Victoria said he pleases me a lot. After dinner, I was in my bedroom taking my clothes off when Victoria got on her knees and started sucking my cock. I held her head as she blew me. That is when I saw her mom watching us with a big smile on her face. I was turned on as she watched her white daughter suck my black cock. After a little bit I said my turn, I threw hot Victoria on the bed. I stimulated and chewed the shit out of her clit. It drove her wild before she came hard then I plunged my black bone deep in her white pussy while her mom watched us smiling.

Victoria whispered my mom is watching so fuck me good. I pounded the shit out of Victoria until she came then I bent her over smack her sexy ass and fucked her some more. I tore her pussy up from behind pulling her hair and nailing her to the bed post until my pleasure volcano erupted in her pleasure palace.

We kissed and held each other lovingly. We both looked and her mom was gone. We went to sleep and woke up both on vacation while her mom is at the apartment. We sat down for breakfast, Veronica said I'm very pleased to see that my daughter is performing her womanly duties for her man.

Victoria said I'm happy you approve of my performing my womanly duties for my boyfriend. I said I'm happy that you are both happy. They both smiled lovingly at me.

The next day, we were sitting around talking when Victoria said oops, I forgot, I have to go shopping with a friend this afternoon. So, she left her mom with me and went out with her friend from work.

I was sitting on the couch chatting with Veronica when I noticed that she was not wearing panties. She had a well-groomed black bush like her daughter. I said wow in my head and my cock skipped a beat.

I excused myself and went to the kitchen. I made myself some tea. I was sipping it enjoying our trillion-dollar view of Silicon Valley. Lost in thought that's when I felt my hard cock being stimulated by a warm mouth.

I looked down and that's when I saw Veronica on her knees performing one of many womanly duties on my cock. I was in shock, I couldn't believe it, but I enjoyed it. There was no way in hell, I was stopping her from blowing me.

I pulled her up and kissed her passionately as I massaged her bush and fingered her pussy. I lifted her up on the counter. I kissed her sweet white thighs and latched on to her clit. I sucked the hell out of her clit as she held my head and enjoyed the pleasure of man.

I kissed my way up to her perky tits just like her daughter's tits. I sucked them and bit them good as she moaned with pleasure. I held her hips and forced my way into her tight pussy. Veronica moaned as I fucked her pussy, she moaned oh god your fucking big and deep in my white pussy.

I pounded Veronica and she held me tight creaming my black cock thoroughly. I could feel it leaking on my balls. I bent Victoria's mom over and penetrated her deep. I pulled her long black hair and punished her pussy properly. She gave up the cream twice as I hammered the shit out of her. I couldn't hold it anymore, so I held her hips firmly and ejaculated all of my warm sperm in her horny cunt.

Veronica said oh my god that was so good no wonder my daughter loves you so much. I said I love your daughter even though I'm deep in her mother. Veronica laughed and said no worries we are a very friendly family. I said it's a total pleasure meeting you and your daughter. Veronica kissed me and we held each other for a while. We hung out on the couch until Victoria came home.

I hugged and kissed Veronica good night and she hugged and kissed Victoria good night. I was asleep when I felt my cock being stroked by Victoria's wonderful hands, I said hello baby you horny and in need of some black dick. Victoria said yeah get on top and pound me baby.

I mounted Victoria and penetrated her deep. I fucked her hard and fast, she held on for dear life as I gave her all the cock she needed. She came twice as I nailed her sexy ass to the bed. I said oh god I love fucking the shit out of you. I held her tight and filled her pussy with my warm sperm.

We held each other tightly and kissed. Victoria said did you enjoy fucking my mother's pussy today while I was out. I said sorry I couldn't help myself. Victoria said its ok I don't mind you fucking my mother with your huge black cock. I said I really liked fucking your mom in the kitchen. I told her how it unfolded, and she smiled. When my mom leaves, my sister is coming to visit next week, she will like your big black cock too. I said oh wow, I look forward to boning your sister too, you are the best girlfriend ever, I love you and Victoria said I love you more.

The end

www.ingramcontent.com/pod-product-compliance
Lightning Source LLC
LaVergne TN
LVHW020545160826
845677LV00015B/4204

* 9 7 9 8 8 1 5 0 2 7 2 3 7 *